NIGHT OF CHAMPIONS

PICK YOUR PATH #2

BY TRACEY WEST

Grosset & Dunlap
An Imprint of Penguin Group (USA) Inc.

GROSSET & DUNLAP
Published by the Penguin Group
Penguin Group (USA) Inc., 375 Hudson Street, New York, New York 10014, USA
Penguin Group (Canada), 90 Eglinton Avenue East, Suite 700,
Toronto, Ontario M4P 2Y3, Canada
(a division of Pearson Penguin Canada Inc.)
Penguin Books Ltd., 80 Strand, London WC2R 0RL, England
Penguin Group Ireland, 25 St. Stephen's Green, Dublin 2, Ireland
(a division of Penguin Books Ltd.)
Penguin Group (Australia), 250 Camberwell Road,
Camberwell, Victoria 3124, Australia
(a division of Pearson Australia Group Pty. Ltd.)
Penguin Books India Pvt. Ltd., 11 Community Centre, Panchsheel Park,
New Delhi—110 017, India
Penguin Group (NZ), 67 Apollo Drive, Rosedale, Auckland 0632, New Zealand
(a division of Pearson New Zealand Ltd.)
Penguin Books (South Africa) (Pty.) Ltd., 24 Sturdee Avenue,
Rosebank, Johannesburg 2196, South Africa

Penguin Books Ltd., Registered Offices: 80 Strand, London WC2R 0RL, England

ISBN 978-0-448-45706-2   10 9 8 7 6 5 4 3 2

"Cody Rhodes has the advantage in this match! He's got The Wrench by the neck and is climbing up to the second rope. Looks like he's going for a bulldog."

The crowd roars as you struggle to get out of Cody's grasp. The Dashing One knocked you into the ring post a few seconds ago and got the upper hand while you were dazed. But you're thinking clearly now.

Cody leaps off the rope and tries to slam you facedown into the ring. But you turn the tables on him and flip him over your shoulders.

BAM! Cody hits the mat hard, and now you're in control of the match. You straddle Cody, grabbing his left leg by the ankle. Then you spin around, twisting his legs like a pretzel.

Cody strains to get out of the leg lock, but they don't call you The Wrench for nothing. When he can't stand the pain any longer, he taps out, and you hear the bell ring throughout the arena.

"And the winner of this match, by submission, is The Wrench!"

A few people in the fourteen-thousand-strong crowd start to clap, but most of them boo. It's not because you're a bad guy. Lately, your fans have been turning against you.

A chant starts to rise in the stands.

"Where's the title? Where's the title? Where's the title?"

You pump your fists in victory over your head, but the crowd doesn't care. You may have won this match, but you've never won a WWE Championship.

It's never bothered you much before. You've been wrestling since you can remember and were a state champion in high school. You joined WWE five years ago, and Mr. McMahon has been impressed with your dedication, your technical skills, and your punishing holds. But you've never managed to win a championship match.

A few months ago, Michael Cole started bringing it up every time you entered the ring. He'd say stuff like, "Here comes The Wrench! Sometimes a loser. Sometimes a winner. Never a champion."

Then it got worse. He started calling you "the Bridesmaid" after that old saying, "Always a bridesmaid, never a bride." The fans loved it. They turned on you faster than Big Show can eat a pepperoni pizza.

So far, you've been keeping your cool and ignoring

him. You didn't get this far in your career by letting what other people say get to you.

Then something comes flying into the ring. Puzzled, you glance down. It looks like a piece of yellow fabric.

Then it hits you—it's a dress. A bridesmaid's dress. Behind the commentators' table, Michael Cole is grinning.

"Here's something to wear in your next match, Bridesmaid!" Cole taunts you.

That's all you can take. You jump out of the ring and storm over to the announcers' table.

WHAM! You lift up the table and flip it over. Michael Cole stumbles backward, and the grin has left his face. You're about to lift him up by the neck, but you stop yourself.

Pounding a coward like Michael Cole won't prove anything. You know what you need to do. You pick a mic up off the floor.

"Listen to me, everybody, and listen good!" you shout. "Ever since I signed with WWE five years ago, I have proven myself worthy of being a Superstar. I give it my all every time I enter the ring."

Some members of the crowd cheer for you.

"But some people think that I need to win a championship to prove myself," you go on. "And it's about time those people shut up. I promise you right here, right now, that I will walk away with a title at the upcoming WWE Night of Champions!"

The crowd goes wild, and you're feeling pumped. You throw down the microphone and exit the arena with your arms raised in victory.

Backstage, the Superstars and crew are all talking about your announcement. You walk past Edge, who gives you a nod.

"It's about time, kid," he says.

Others aren't so nice. Alberto Del Rio bursts out laughing when he sees you.

"I'll make you a bet, Wrench," he says. "After you lose at WWE Night of Champions, you have to wear that yellow dress."

"I'm not going to lose," you say confidently, but inside you're hit with a blast of doubt. Now everybody's going to be watching you. If you don't win a championship at the big pay-per-view event, you'll never hear the end of it.

You try to sleep that night, but every time you close your eyes, you hear the crowd chanting, "Where's the title? Where's the title?" Early the next morning, you get a message on your phone asking you to fly to WWE headquarters immediately. Mr. McMahon wants to see you.

"Here's the deal," Mr. McMahon tells you from his seat behind his large desk. "I like you, kid. It's about time you stood up for yourself. So I have an opportunity for you."

You lean forward, curious.

"R-Truth wants you to become his tag team partner," Mr. McMahon continues. "You could compete for the World Tag Team Championship. I'll approve your move from *SmackDown* to *Raw*."

You think about it. R-Truth has already been a United States Championship winner. Why would he want to team with a Superstar like you, who's got something to prove?

"What if I stay in *SmackDown*?" you ask.

"Then you could compete for a shot at one of the bigger championships," Mr. McMahon replies. "But to be honest, kid, you might not want to aim so big on your first shot. I think you and R-Truth have a good chance of winning the tag team title."

If you stay in *SmackDown*, go to page 29.

If you leave for *Raw* to team with R-Truth, go to page 41.

Normally, dirty tactics like these aren't your style. But they might be the only way you can win.

"All right," you say. "Do what you want. And thanks."

When it's time for the match, you get called to the ring first. When Big Show enters, the fans start cheering wildly. They're expecting him to demolish you, and they can't wait.

It's a good thing I agreed to let The New Nexus help, you think as the starting bell rings. Big Show just stands there, staring at you. You take a deep breath. You might as well get things started.

You charge toward Big Show, hitting him with a clothesline. Someone smaller might have gone down, but not Big Show. He just watches you with an amused expression on his face.

Next you try climbing the ropes. You're not usually a high-flier, but you're going to need some extra momentum to make an impact with Big Show.

As you soar across the ring, Big Show grabs you in midair. Then he lifts you high above his head, ready to slam you into the mat. You think you can turn things around by swinging your legs around his head . . .

That's when David Otunga and Mason Ryan race into the ring. Big Show tosses you behind his back and grabs each one of The New Nexus Superstars by the neck.

BAM! He slams the two of them together and then drops them on the mat. Terrified, they run away.

"Good luck, Wrench!" Ryan calls behind him.

You're on the mat, groaning. Big Show picks you up again, powerslams you, and covers you for the pin. You've lost the match—and your chance to face Randy Orton for the WWE Championship.

THE END

You snap out of your daydream of challenging Randy Orton. How do you expect to beat a legendary Superstar like him?

That night, you and R-Truth fly to Nashville, where you'll be competing on *Raw* in just two days.

You and R-Truth practice for hours in a gym near the Nashville arena. By the time Monday night rolls around, you're ready for your match.

Backstage, you're ready to go in your gray trunks and matching boots. R-Truth is jogging in place, building up energy for the match. You can hear the commentators through the backstage speakers.

"The winners of our next match are competing for a chance at the WWE Tag Team Championship!" Michael Cole says. "John Morrison and Daniel Bryan are facing off against R-Truth and The Wrench."

"The Wrench?" Jerry Lawler laughs. "What's a champion like R-Truth doing with a loser like that guy?"

"Last week The Wrench promised every fan that he was going to walk away with a title at the WWE Night of Champions," Michael Cole replies. "Tonight we'll see if he's got the skills to back it up."

Your fists clench, and an angry look crosses your face.

"Don't let them get to you," R-Truth tells you. "They get paid to talk trash. I know you're not a loser."

When the match starts, R-Truth jumps in the ring with John Morrison. The Monday Night Delight is a confident Superstar with wavy brown hair. He goes after R-Truth aggressively. The rapping Superstar gets caught off guard, then turns the tables on Morrison and lifts him up to perform a powerslam. But he's near Morrison's corner, and Daniel Bryan tags in. He attacks R-Truth with a series of vicious elbow strikes, driving him into the corner.

R-Truth tags you, and you jump in to face Daniel Bryan. You use your momentum to deliver a hard kick to his chest, and he staggers back.

Then the blond wrestler charges into you, sending you slamming into the ropes. He yanks you by the arm and stands behind you, getting ready to trap you in a hold.

You push away, tagging R-Truth in the process. He runs back in the ring and spars with Daniel Bryan. Bryan tags out, and Morrison is in the ring again. You think R-Truth may tag you, but he doesn't even look tired.

He propels himself off the ropes, spins like a corkscrew, and then slams his arm into Morrison's chest.

"It's the Lie Detector!" Jerry Lawler yells.

R-Truth's move sends Morrison to the mat, and the rapping Superstar covers him for the pin. The crowd is on their feet yelling, "What's up?"

"R-Truth and The Wrench take the match—no thanks to The Wrench," Michael Cole says, insulting you.

His words continue to sting you as you head backstage. You should be happy—but you're starting to feel lost in R-Truth's shadow.

That night, Skip Sheffield of The New Nexus approaches you.

"Dude, as long as R-Truth is around, you won't get to do anything," he tells you. "You should join The New Nexus and tag team with me instead."

If you stick with R-Truth, go to page 35.

If you team with Sheffield, go to page 90.

You decide that proving to everyone you can beat Alberto Del Rio is more important than winning a championship. Backstage, you ask him for another shot.

"You had your chance," he says, brushing past you. "You're just not worthy of facing a superior athlete like me."

The Superstar's attitude really gets to you. At the end of *SmackDown*, Kofi Kingston calls out Del Rio for a match the following week, and Del Rio accepts. You know what you need to do.

The next week you wait backstage to make your move. Halfway through the match, Del Rio knocks out Kofi with a powerful suplex. Then he backs up against the ropes so he can catapult off them and finish off Kofi for good.

That's when you rush up behind Del Rio and drag him underneath the ropes by his ankles. After he crashes to the floor, you hit him on the back with a chair and run away. Kofi comes to and drags Del Rio back in the ring, pinning him for the win.

Now Kofi Kingston is the number one contender for the Intercontinental Championship, and he owes it to you. Maybe he'll give you a shot at the contender slot.

Go to page 81.

"When Mr. McMahon signed me to a *SmackDown* contract, he saw the champion in me," Drew barks into the mic. "He made me the Chosen One, and I didn't let him down. I've been a champion before, and tonight, I'll be a champion again!"

The crowd cheers wildly, and you clench your fists anxiously. You decide to go for it—run for the ladder before he knows what's happening and grab that championship.

At the sound of the bell, you race to the ladder while McIntyre is still playing up to the crowd. The crowd starts yelling at McIntyre, and he turns to see you when you're two steps from the top. He charges at the ladder like an angry bull, knocking it over.

You plummet ten feet and crash hard onto the mat. The next thing you know, Drew McIntyre is holding up the United States Championship triumphantly. You've lost your chance at a title!

THE END

Since Randy Orton is still recovering from Cena's assault, you decide to target him first. You rush him, smashing him into the corner turnbuckle.

But Orton isn't as dazed as you think. He charges at you with an angry growl, jumps in the air, and then wraps his hands around your neck on the way down. You crash hard into the mat.

"It's the RKO! This is the end for The Wrench!" Jerry Lawler calls out.

He's right. Randy Orton pins you easily. You leave the ring and head backstage. Surprisingly, none of the other Superstars give you a hard time. You might not have won a title, but you've proven yourself by taking down a lot of guys.

Backstage, you watch Cena bring down Orton with an Attitude Adjustment from the second rope. You watch enviously as he wraps the WWE Championship around his waist. That could have been you!

THE END

"Wrench! Tag me in!" R-Truth calls from the corner.

You ignore him, jumping to your feet to face Mark Henry. He lumbers toward you, and you jump up, twisting your body so you can smack him in the chest with the soles of both feet.

"Whoa! Nice dropkick!" Jerry Lawler says.

But Mark Henry just stands there. You punch him a few times, but he swats you away like a fly. Then he wraps his arms around you and squeezes you tight.

"Oh no! It's a Bear Hug! The Wrench is in trouble!" Lawler wails. Mark Henry swings you back and forth like a rag doll. By the time he drops you to the mat, you're done. Mark Henry easily covers you for the pin. Evan Bourne races into the ring to celebrate with his partner—they're going to Tag Team Turmoil.

And you're not. You stand up, aching, and slowly walk to the corner. R-Truth is shaking his head.

"I told you to tag me, man!"

THE END

A little voice inside you is whispering. *If you're going to do this, go big.* Winning the United States Championship would really quiet your doubting fans. And part of you is curious to know what Mr. McMahon has in mind for you.

"I want a shot at Drew McIntyre," you tell the chairman.

Mr. McMahon looks thoughtful. Then he leans forward. "Tell you what," he says. "I'll leave it up to you. You've got two choices. Here's the first one: Defeat Undertaker, and I'll let you face McIntyre at the WWE Night of Champions."

Undertaker? The thought makes you turn paler than Sheamus.

"Um, what's the second choice?" you ask.

"Well, you're not the only one who wants to take on Drew," Mr. McMahon replies. "There are three other Superstars who want the title as much as you do. I'll set you up in a specialty match against each one of them. Take 'em all down, and you've got your shot."

You're stunned. Leaving things up to Mr. McMahon

was a big risk, and now you've got a decision to make. Face Undertaker, a practically undefeatable tower of terror, or trample a trio of unknown title hopefuls.

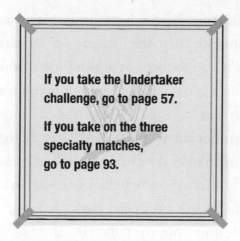

If you take the Undertaker challenge, go to page 57.

If you take on the three specialty matches, go to page 93.

A Cobra Clutch is a submission hold that you do with both athletes on their feet. Randy Orton is powerfully strong, so it's probably not a good idea. You'll have a better chance getting him to submit if you can get him on the mat first.

You gather all your strength and charge at him, clotheslining him in the chest with an outstretched arm. It's a good hit, and you're in luck because Orton is close to the ropes. He's propelled backward and flips over the bottom rope onto the concrete.

But just when you think the action is over, John Cena races into the ring and knocks down the ref. Then he jumps over the ropes and throws Orton into the ring. He's not happy about being eliminated, and he's taking it out on his old rival.

He pounds Orton like a punching bag until he sees the ref start to stir. Before the ref gets up, Cena slides out of the ring.

Now Orton is on the mat where you want him, and you make your move. You force his legs down over his chest as you keep pressure on his shoulders for the three count.

Orton struggles, but you hold fast.

"One . . . two . . . three!" the ref calls out.

You fall backward, stunned. You've done it! Not only are you a champion—you're the WWE Champion!

You slide out of the ring and grab the championship. Then you jump back in and hold it up over your head, letting the cheers of the crowd wash over you.

"The Wrench has done it!" Jerry Lawler cries, amazed. "He's the WWE Champion! Nobody can give him a hard time again!"

You got that right! you think. You're not sure how long you'll hold the title—Orton and Cena are sure to come gunning for you—but right now, it's yours. And it feels great!

THE END

Orton is trying to distract you—and it works.

"Let's do this!" you yell, and slide under the ropes to face him.

The Viper moves so fast, you don't have time to react. He turns so that his back faces yours and then reaches back to grab your neck with his right arm. Then he twists around and drops, pounding you into the cement floor.

"It's an Inverted Headlock Backbreaker!" Jerry Lawler cries. "The Wrench may not recover from this!"

"He'd better do something soon because the ref is about to count him out," Michael Cole chimes in.

That's when you realize—you've left your match with Sheamus! You try to run back into the ring, but Orton blocks your path.

"Nine . . . ten!" the ref counts, and the bell rings. The match is over—and you've lost. Randy Orton tricked you, and you fell for it.

Randy Orton smiles. "That was easier than taking candy from a baby!"

THE END

"Aided Superbomb," you tell R-Truth, and he climbs to the top rope and sits.

You've got to move fast. You've got only five seconds before the ref counts you out. You push Kidd forward so that he's facing R-Truth. Then you put your head under his right arm and lift him up, swinging his legs onto R-Truth's shoulders. R-Truth grabs Kidd's legs so he can't kick out.

R-Truth stands up and jumps. You move out of the way, and Tyson Kidd collides with the mat.

You race to your corner just in time. R-Truth covers Tyson Kidd, pinning down his chest. The ref counts out, "One . . . two . . . three!"

"YEAH!" you yell, jumping into the ring. You grab R-Truth's wrist and raise your arms into the air.

"The winners of this contest and the new WWE Tag Team Champions . . . R-Truth and The Wrench!"

Tyson Kidd rolls out of the ring, and he and David Hart Smith walk away, shaking their heads. That's okay with you. This moment is all about you and your tag team partner.

You take the mic from the ring announcer. "So many of you didn't have faith in me! But I did it! I am a champion!"

The crowd cheers and starts to chant your name. "Wrench! Wrench! Wrench!"

R-Truth grins at you. "I knew you could do it, man."

THE END

You decide to give it everything you've got. You lunge at Punk and deliver a barrage of punches so fast that he can't make a move.

Then . . . *BAM!* You smack him with a spinning kick to the chin, and Punk goes down.

In a flash you're on him, flipping him over so he's facedown on the mat. You sit on his back and grab his neck in a chin lock, pulling back, straining his head and neck. You've got him in a Camel Clutch, one of your favorite submission holds.

But all that fast action has tapped you of your strength, and Punk manages to free his arms. He pushes up forcefully from the mat, sending you flying backward. He's broken the hold!

Punk races to the corner and climbs the ropes. He grabs them and pulls back hard, propelling himself over the ring and right over your head! As he lands behind you, he knocks you down on the mat.

He jumps down next to you and pulls your right arm back, then loops his arms around your arm and head in a tight grip.

"It's the Anaconda Vise!" Michael Cole cries out.

You know you're in trouble. Punk pulls your head and shoulders forward, and the pain in your arm and neck are unbearable. You try to kick out of the hold, but it's no use. Your head is starting to feel fuzzy and your eyesight is blurry . . .

"And the winner of this contest is CM Punk!"

The tight grip around you releases, and you sit up, stunned. You tapped out, and you didn't even realize it. Then it hits you—you've lost your championship shot. It's all over.

But it's not all bad. When you get back to your hotel room that night, you see that the wrestling blogs are on fire. Everyone is impressed with you for taking on three Superstars in one night. You might not have a title, but the taunting from the fans stops from here on out.

THE END

Randy Orton's challenge scares you. There's something behind his smile that tells you he's not going to make this easy for you.

"The Wrench doesn't jump through hoops for anyone," you say boldly, trying to put a positive spin on backing out. "This challenge was for you, not for one of your loser friends."

Orton's smile disappears. "Forget about it, Wrench. And you'd better get out of here fast, before I decide to teach you a lesson."

You quickly run off the stage, grateful that you're still in one piece. R-Truth is looking at you, shaking his head.

"Well, I tried," you say. "Guess we'll have to go for the tag team title."

"No way," R-Truth says. "I thought you had guts. But ditching me was not cool. And you just showed everyone what a coward you are. This partnership is over."

R-Truth walks away—along with your hopes of winning a championship. You've really messed things up.

THE END

R-Truth runs back into the ring to face Jey Uso. While the ref has his eyes on them, you climb into the ring and sneak behind him. But Jimmy Uso sees you.

"Ref, behind you!" he calls out.

The ref spins around just as your fist is making contact with his shoulder. He's furious. The bell rings, and the ref walks to the announcers' booth.

"And the winners, due to disqualification, are the Usos!"

R-Truth is more embarrassed than angry.

"When Tamina interfered, I was furious," he says. "I should have just let it go. Sorry, man."

"That's okay," you say, and you mean it—even though your hopes of a championship have been dashed. But R-Truth is smiling.

"How about we challenge whoever wins tonight to a title match?" he asks.

"I'm in," you say. "And next time, we'll do it right."

THE END

You decide there's no way you can trust R-Truth. Besides, you know there are bigger championships up for grabs if you stay in *SmackDown*.

"I think I'll stay in *SmackDown*, if that's okay," you tell Mr. McMahon. "Drew McIntyre's got the United States Championship. And Dolph Ziggler is the Intercontinental Champion. Both of them will be facing challengers at WWE Night of Champions, right? I'd like that challenger to be me."

Mr. McMahon raises an eyebrow. "Now, hold on there," he says. "I know you, Wrench, and you know better than that. Nobody gets a championship shot unless they earn it."

"Okay," you say, looking directly into the chairman's steely eyes. "I want this. Bad. What do I have to do?"

Mr. McMahon leans back in his leather chair, thoughtful.

"Alberto Del Rio is the number one contender for the Intercontinental Championship," he says. "If you want a shot at Ziggler, you'll have to face Del Rio first."

You remember how Del Rio taunted you yesterday,

and your fists clench. It would be satisfying to take him down. But you've faced Del Rio twice before, and once you lost badly. Taking him down might be tough.

"As for the United States Championship shot, I need to think about that more," Mr. McMahon tells you. "If you decide to go after McIntyre, how you get there will be up to me."

You're not sure what to do. You could get in the ring with someone you know—or leave your fate in the hands of Mr. McMahon.

If you go after the United States Championship, go to page 18.

If you face Del Rio at the Intercontinental Championship, go to page 49.

You've seen enough Ladder Matches to know that it's a mistake to climb the ladder until you've knocked out your opponent—that way he can't go after you. Taking down this six-foot-five Superstar won't be easy, but it's what you've got to do.

When the bell rings, you charge forward, thinking you'll bring down McIntyre. But before you can get close, his right foot makes contact with your forehead, and you stumble back.

"The Scotsman's starting off the match with a Big Boot to The Wrench's head!" the announcer calls out. "That's gotta hurt!"

You're mad at yourself—you should have known that McIntyre would use his height advantage against you like that.

McIntyre looks pretty pleased with himself, and that gives you an idea. You charge at him again, and McIntyre, thinking you're being stupid, tries to kick you again. But this time you're ready. You grab his leg and try to flip him. He resists, but you've got him off balance, and that's good.

The match goes on like this for a while. McIntyre goes after you with power moves, and you avoid most of them. When you can, you hit him with a surprise round kick or unexpected punch. But no matter how hard you try, you can't get him down.

Then McIntyre manages to grab you in a face lock, and he falls back on the mat, sending you crashing into the mat face-first. The suplex knocks the wind out of you, but you're not out.

Then it hits you—McIntyre doesn't know that. You close your eyes, pretending to be out cold.

McIntyre goes for the bait. He starts to climb the ladder, and the crowd's going wild. That's when you spring up and pull him off the ladder, throwing him down to the mat. This is your chance to knock him out, so you can climb the ladder.

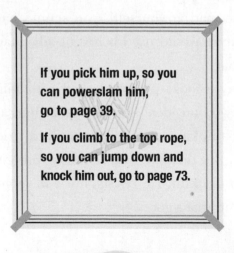

If you pick him up, so you
can powerslam him,
go to page 39.

If you climb to the top rope,
so you can jump down and
knock him out, go to page 73.

CONTINUED FROM PAGE 76

While the offer from The New Nexus seems nice, it's not your style. You're either going to win on your own or fail on your own.

The announcer calls your name, and you head to the ring first. Then it's Big Show's turn. The fans in the stands are yelling and stomping their feet. They want to see him crush you. It's not that they don't like you—they just want to witness the spectacle.

After just two minutes in the ring, you find yourself in trouble. Big Show lifts you high above his head, ready to slam you into the mat. But you think you can turn things around by swinging your legs around his head.

It works! You still go down, but you're able to take Big Show with you and control how you land. Big Show looks surprised. Suddenly, you feel confident.

The match rages on for at least ten minutes. Big Show keeps trying to pick you up and slam you, but you manage to take control of the situation almost every time. He does pound you on the mat a few times, but you quickly roll away and get to your feet.

In the end, you get lucky when one of your kicks

sends Big Show's head crashing into the turnbuckle. He slumps to the mat, and you pin him for the win. You almost can't believe it.

You're standing there, stunned, when Randy Orton walks into the ring.

"I'm not sure if it was luck or skill that helped you tonight," he said. "But you've still got two more Superstars to defeat. Next time, you'll face Yoshi Tatsu on *Raw*."

When you face Yoshi Tatsu a few days later, the Japanese Superstar gets you in an Octopus hold. His leg is draped around your neck, and all his weight is putting pressure on you. You're not sure how you're going to get out of this one.

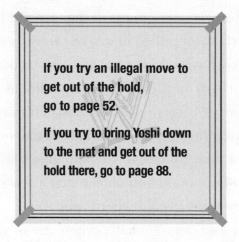

If you try an illegal move to get out of the hold, go to page 52.

If you try to bring Yoshi down to the mat and get out of the hold there, go to page 88.

"Um, no thanks," you tell Skip Sheffield. You promised yourself you'd stay focused. Breaking up a successful tag team now would be a mistake.

The next day you get a call from Mr. McMahon. "There's going to be a Tag Team Turmoil match at WWE Night of Champions," he tells you, and you start to get excited. In a Turmoil match, four tag teams compete at once. "There's one slot left. On the next *Raw*, you and R-Truth are going to face Mark Henry and Evan Bourne for it."

"Thanks, Mr. McMahon," you say.

As you flip your phone closed, you think about what's in store. Evan Bourne is a high-flying Superstar who's about your size. It might be tough getting him in your grasp long enough for a submission hold, but not impossible.

Mark Henry, the "World's Strongest Man," is a powerful juggernaut who could probably squeeze you like a grape if he wanted to. You're glad you won't have to face him alone.

Before the match, you and R-Truth work out some

strategies. "If you end up alone in the ring with Mark Henry, tag me in," he advises. "If we work fast, we can use the five count after you tag me to take him down together."

You nod. It sounds like a pretty good plan.

"This is gonna be a good one tonight," Jerry Lawler says right before your match. "I can't wait to see The Wrench try to put one of his holds on Mark Henry. He won't be able to get his arms around him!"

"That's if The Wrench even gets in the ring," Michael Cole adds. "He'll probably just let R-Truth handle this like he did last time."

Just like before, Cole's words cut right through you. R-Truth smiles and waves at the fans when you walk to the ring, but you stomp out with an angry look on your face.

When the bell rings, you jump into the ring without even a nod to R-Truth. You've got something to prove, and nobody's going to stop you.

Evan Bourne climbs through the ropes and charges at you.

BAM! You immediately clothesline him, and he falls back. He jumps back on his feet quickly and climbs the ropes, flying off them so that he can crush you. You grab him in midair and slam him onto the mat.

You get on the mat with him and grab him in a chin lock. Bourne struggles against it, slowly inching his way across the mat until he reaches his corner. Then he tags Mark Henry.

The big wrestler climbs through the ropes and stomps after you. The whole ring shakes. You remember what R-Truth told you to do, but you're feeling strong and confident. If you take on Mark Henry by yourself, Michael Cole and Jerry Lawler will have no choice but to stop picking on you.

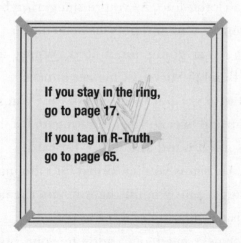

If you stay in the ring, go to page 17.

If you tag in R-Truth, go to page 65.

"No, thanks," you tell CM Punk. "I can do this myself."

You get to your feet, still reeling from the Oklahoma Stampede. But you're not about to give up now. With all your might, you shove Swagger into the ropes. If you can get this muscled monster on the mat, you'll have an advantage.

But Swagger bounces off the ropes and pummels you with a clothesline. As you're staggering backward, he spins you around and puts his head under your arm.

"Swagger is going for a Red, White, and Blue Thunder Bomb!" Michael Cole announces.

You try to get out of his grasp, but you can't. He flips you up and over so you are sitting on his shoulders. Then he spins around and jumps forward.

BAM! He slams you backward into the mat. You're done. Swagger pins you for the win, and the next thing you hear is the buzzing of a razor . . .

The shaved head only adds to your humiliation. Maybe you should have asked CM Punk for help after all.

THE END

You're about eighty pounds lighter than McIntyre, so climbing the ropes seems like the smart move. But you don't want to give him the chance to move. You face McIntyre and pull him to his feet. Then you reach underneath him and get ready to lift him up on top of your shoulders.

You'll need a burst of superstrength to do it. You look up at the shining gold championship hanging above you, and the desire to win fills you. With a groan, you hoist McIntyre onto your shoulders.

WHAM! After a running start, you fall forward, slamming McIntyre's back hard into the mat. His eyes are closed, and he's barely moving. This is your chance.

You scramble up the ladder as quickly as you can. Down below, you see McIntyre get to his feet. You've got to move fast.

You reach up and . . . you've got it! At that exact moment McIntyre knocks the ladder out from under your feet! You plummet down and land on top of the fallen ladder.

Every cell in your body hurts—but you don't care.

You've got the United States Championship in your hands, and nobody can take it from you. At least—not tonight.

Drew McIntyre storms out of the ring, leaving you to slowly get to your feet. You raise your arms in the air, holding the gleaming prize above your head.

"Wrench! Wrench! Wrench! Wrench!"

The crowd chants your name over and over, and you love the sound of it. It's great to be a champion!

THE END

"I think I'll team with R-Truth," you tell Mr. McMahon, and he smiles, pleased. R-Truth has a good record as a tag team partner. Teaming with him might be your best chance for a title.

"Excellent!" Mr. McMahon says. "On Saturday we're doing a special event for soldiers and their families. I want both of you there to announce the new tag team."

"Thanks, Mr. McMahon," you say. "I won't let you down."

It turns out the event is going to be a big outdoor barbecue in Texas, with bands playing and appearances by WWE Superstars. You and R-Truth meet up for the first time in a wardrobe trailer on the scene. The rapping Superstar is wearing jeans and a black T-shirt emblazoned with WHAT'S UP? His short dreadlocks frame his face.

"Hey, man, thanks for letting me team with you," you say, shaking his hand. "To be honest, I'm not exactly sure why you asked me."

"I like your attitude," R-Truth replies. "The other

night, you sounded like someone who wants to win. I'm ready for another championship myself. I've got a good feeling about this."

You nod. "Me too," you say.

Pretty soon the trailer is swarming with Superstars as everyone gets ready for the event. The whole thing's going to be filmed for TV. Soon it's time for you and R-Truth to make your announcement.

You exit the trailer, and an assistant in a WWE polo shirt leads you to the stage. As you approach, you can see the excited crowd. Many men and women are wearing uniforms, and there are lots of kids there, too. You see a lot of fans with R-Truth signs, but nobody has a sign that says THE WRENCH.

The crowd goes wild as you and R-Truth climb onstage. They're chanting, "What's up?"

R-Truth grabs the mic first. He's got a ton of charisma, and the crowd loves him.

"It's great to be here on this beautiful day!" he cries, and the crowd cheers and claps. "I'm here today with my friend Wrench to make a big announcement: We are teaming up to take the WWE Tag Team Championship title at WWE Night of Champions!"

The applause is deafening. You take the microphone from him and try to talk. The crowd is chanting R-Truth's name over and over. He flashes them a dazzling smile and waves.

You're starting to feel a little left out standing in R-Truth's shadow. You leave the stage without saying anything.

"You okay?" R-Truth asks, but you don't answer.

Then it's Randy Orton's turn to talk to the crowd, and the Viper's got an announcement, too.

"Mr. McMahon is making me put my WWE Championship on the line at WWE Night of Champions," Orton says. "He thinks that there's a Superstar out there worthy of stealing my title. I say, prove it!"

Suddenly you get a crazy idea. What if you ran up to the mic and challenged Randy Orton right here, right now? That would be awesome.

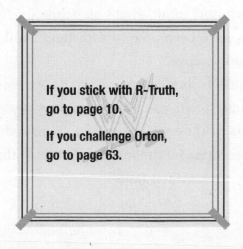

If you stick with R-Truth,
go to page 10.

If you challenge Orton,
go to page 63.

You decide not to try a submission hold on CM Punk until you've regained some of your energy. You counter with a few spinning kicks of your own, and you get him off balance. He runs to the ropes and bounces back fiercely, trying to knock you down with a clothesline. But you're quick, and you dodge out of the way.

You try to take him down with another kick, but he grabs your leg before it hits him. He shoves you down hard onto the mat. Then he picks you up over his head and drapes you over his shoulders.

"CM Punk is going for the GTS!" the announcer crows, and you know what's in store for you. Few Superstars have been able to withstand Punk's Go To Sleep finishing move.

You quickly slide down and wrap your legs around Punk's chest. Then you twist your legs, sending you both down to the mat. Punk was surprised by your comeback, and he hit the mat hard. Now is the perfect time to try a submission hold.

If you try to finish with a
sharpshooter, go to page 69.

If you use a Figure-Four
Leglock, go to page 80.

Rey Mysterio uses the ropes to propel himself toward you, and you stop him with a clothesline. As he staggers back, you quickly pick him up and turn him upside down. He's smaller than you, so it's not hard to do. Then you fall forward on top of him, slamming him into the mat.

As you fall, Mysterio knocks into John Cena, who's got Randy Orton cornered. An angry Cena spins around and picks up Mysterio, lifting him up over his head.

BAM! Mysterio goes down hard, and Cena covers him for the pin. Randy Orton breaks out of the corner and starts to shake off the haze that Cena put on him. You're one man closer to getting the championship title, but you've got to take out Cena and Orton first.

If you go after Orton, go to page 16.

If you go after Cena, go to page 71.

You nod to CM Punk, and he nods back. As you try to get to your feet, your body aching, Punk slithers into the ring like a snake and grabs the ref by the ankles. He crashes into the ring. He's out cold! Punk tosses him onto the arena floor and then disappears.

Jack Swagger turns around. He sees the ref is missing, but he's not sure what happened.

Behind him, CM Punk jumps into the ring. He grabs Swagger's head with one hand and then hurtles forward, driving Swagger's face into the mat.

Swagger is down and dazed. CM Punk slides out of the ring. You move quickly, flipping Swagger on his back and covering him for the pin.

You're in luck because the ref is recovered and back in the ring just in time. He counts out Swagger. "One . . . two . . . three!"

The ref raises your arm in the air, but you're not done yet. You take an electric razor and shave half of Swagger's blond hair before he shakes you off. He's a sore loser, but you don't care. You've won your first specialty match!

When you get backstage, Theodore Long tells you that you'll be fighting your next match the same night. This one's a Falls Count Anywhere Match against Chris "The Masterpiece" Masters. This conceited Superstar has a devastating submission hold, the Master Lock.

Soon after the match begins, you slide out of the ring. It's a Falls Count Anywhere Match, so you can pin your opponent anywhere inside (or even outside) the building.

Masters jumps over the ropes and charges after you. You spot a chair nearby. It could be just what you need—although playing dirty isn't normally your style.

If you quickly get back in the ring, go to page 56.

If you hit Masters with the chair, go to page 84.

Now is your chance to face Albert Del Rio. The *Raw* crowd boos as Alberto Del Rio walks into the arena in the gold trunks and white scarf he always wears. When the announcer calls your name, you expect to hear a lot of cheers. But the crowd is down on you, too.

"Where's the title? Where's the title?"

Del Rio is too busy grinning and waving at the crowd and doesn't even acknowledge you when you enter. He's about two inches taller than you, and for a second you wonder if you're going to be able to take him down.

"The winner of this contest will advance to the WWE Night of Champions for an Intercontinental Championship match against Dolph Ziggler!" the announcer proclaims, and the crowd goes wild.

Ding! Ding! Ding!

When the bell rings, Del Rio is still busy flashing his blinding white smile at the crowd. You run up to him and clothesline him in the chest with your right arm, sending him flying back into the corner.

Now you've got his attention—and he's fighting

mad. He charges toward you like an angry bull and grabs you around the chest so he can perform a punishing suplex. But you twist out of his grasp, delivering a side kick to his chin as you jump away.

Del Rio staggers back, stunned by the blow. You kick him again, this time in the chest, and he falls backward on the mat. You quickly apply a Figure-Four Leglock, hoping he'll submit just like Cody Rhodes did in your last match.

But Del Rio kicks his way out of the hold, sending you sprawling back. You jump to your feet, and the two of you exchange blows. The match is an even contest for a while, until Del Rio manages to get his hands around your neck.

"It's time for the Rio Grande!" he announces with a smile.

Before you can react, he swings his legs up around you, and you both go crashing to the mat. Then he twists his legs around your neck, pinning you down.

You know the move, and Del Rio is a master at it. No matter how hard you struggle, you can't break out of the hold. With your last ounce of strength, you tap the mat.

He jumps to his feet and sneers down at you. "Better luck next time, Bridesmaid!"

You can't believe you just lost. There goes your shot at the Intercontinental Championship!

Go to page 13.

Every muscle in your body is straining, and you can't think clearly. You can't see the ref, so you decide to do the only thing within your reach—you jab your fist right in Yoshi's eye.

He cries out and drops you on the mat. Perfect! There's only one problem—the ref was standing right there. You just couldn't see him.

"You're *out*!" he cries, and the final bell rings.

"And the winner of this match, due to a disqualification, is Yoshi Tatsu!"

You quietly leave the ring, defeated. It looks like you won't be facing Randy Orton at the WWE Night of Champions.

THE END

Even though you're a pro at submission holds, you don't want to turn your back on Cody's partner, Ted DiBiase. You decide to go for the flying lariat—but you have to act fast.

You run to the ropes and climb up. Then you jump off, wrapping your arm around Cody's neck as you make contact.

BAM! Your momentum pushes him straight down onto the mat. Cody is dazed. You get down on the mat and flip him over, pinning down his shoulders. The ref starts to count.

"One . . . two . . ."

Cody kicks out! You almost had him—and now you want to finish him even more. He's angry, and he comes at you with a hard kick to the chest. It sends you reeling back, but you're not out.

You charge forward, smacking Cody hard. Then you wrap your arm around his neck, tightening your grip so he can't get out. Once the face lock is secure, you sweep your legs against his, knocking him off his feet as you drop down to the ring.

WHAM! It's a sound DDT, and Cody is dazed once again. You try to pin him a second time.

"One . . . two . . . three!" the ref counts.

The crowd goes crazy. You and R-Truth have won your second match in the Tag Team Turmoil! You're one match away from the title.

"The Wrench really took control out there!" the commentator says.

But you and R-Truth barely have time to recover before the arena lights dim and the Hart Dynasty makes its way to the ring. Tyson Kidd and David Hart Smith look fresh and ready to go.

R-Truth steps into the ring first to give you a chance to recover from your bout with Cody Rhodes. David Hart Smith charges from his corner like a bull, picking up R-Truth and driving him into the mat with a dynamic suplex. For a second it looks like he might pin your partner, but R-Truth is tough. He jumps to his feet and counters with a jumping calf kick.

Smith grunts as R-Truth's foot makes contact, and the rapping Superstar goes for another one. This time, Smith grabs his ankle and pulls R-Truth toward him. Then he lifts him up for another suplex.

R-Truth kicks out, and he's close enough to the corner to tag you. You know you have to get Smith to the mat before he has a chance to pick you up, so you ram into him like a speeding train.

Smith goes flying back into his corner and tags Tyson Kidd. He attacks you with a series of powerful kicks, hitting you pretty hard. But you manage to grab his arms behind his back and twist them into a hold. You've got the advantage—but not for long.

You're near your corner, so you tag R-Truth and give him a nod. The two of you have been practicing some two-man moves. Now it's time to bust one out.

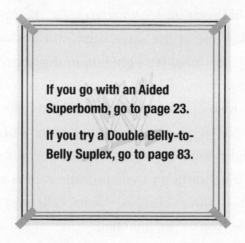

If you go with an Aided Superbomb, go to page 23.

If you try a Double Belly-to-Belly Suplex, go to page 83.

CONTINUED FROM PAGE 48

You just can't bring yourself to hit Chris Masters with a folding chair. You're an athlete at heart, and that seems like cheating to you. You sneak past Masters so you can climb back into the ring.

WHACK! Masters has the same idea you had, and he clocks *you* hard on the head with a folding chair. As you wobble back and forth, dazed, he stands behind you and puts his arms under your armpits, then pulls your arms back while at the same time pushing your head down on your chest. He's got you in the Master Lock!

It's a submission hold you really admire, but right now you wish it wasn't being used on you. Masters knows he has to pin you to win this, so he waits until he sees the lights fade in your eyes before he lets go. Then he lifts you up and slams you into the concrete floor.

"One . . . two . . . three!" the ref calls, and you hear the terrible ring of the final bell.

"The Wrench is finished! Chris Masters is going on to face the next opponent!"

Next time, I'll use that chair! you tell yourself.

THE END

Defeating Undertaker may be the most difficult thing you've attempted in your life. But you have no idea which three Superstars Mr. McMahon plans to put you up against. If you choose Undertaker, you'll only have to win once.

"I'll try Undertaker," you say.

Mr. McMahon looks surprised. "You've got a lot of nerve, kid. I'm liking the new you. So you got it. You can face Undertaker on the next *SmackDown*."

The wrestling blogs light up with comments once the match is announced.

"The Wrench has built a reputation for being a steady, coolheaded Superstar. But this latest move makes me wonder if The Wrench has a screw loose!"

You decide to ignore the blogs and focus on the match. By the next *SmackDown*, you're ready.

"The following contest is a one fall!" the announcer blares. "Approaching the ring, weighing in at one hundred seventy pounds, is The Wrench!"

To your surprise, the crowd cheers you. They must like your brave move.

You jump up on the ropes and wave to your fans. Then the arena goes black.

Bong. Bong. Bong. Bong.

A mournful bell tolls, and organ music plays.

"And now approaching the ring, weighing in at two hundred ninety-nine pounds, is Undertaker!"

Your blood runs cold as Undertaker slowly makes his way down the aisle, bathed in midnight-blue light. He steps into the ring, removes his long, black leather coat, and faces you.

Ding! Ding! Ding! At the sound of the bell, you race forward, your heart pumping. You strike Undertaker with your most powerful round kick.

Undertaker doesn't flinch. He lifts you up, turns you upside down, and then drops to his knees, slamming you into the ring. You're helpless as Undertaker pins you to the mat.

You're devastated by the loss, but you feel better after you see the text Mr. McMahon has sent you:

Your match with Undertaker really spiked your popularity, kid. I'll give you another title shot at the next pay-per-view.

So you have to wait. And next time, if you have a choice, you won't choose Undertaker.

THE END

You realize that Orton is trying to distract you. On some level, that's flattering. He wouldn't be trying to do that unless he was worried about you. But you don't take the bait.

You keep sparring with Sheamus. Outside the ring, Orton doesn't let up.

"Come on, Wrench! Get out here and prove yourself!" he taunts you.

You keep ignoring him, and then you realize that he's making Sheamus furious. He rushes to the corner and leans over to yell at Orton.

"Get out of here and let the king take care of this!" he bellows.

You realize that Sheamus is the one who's distracted, and that gives you an advantage. You grab his arm, climb to the top rope, and then springboard backward, taking Sheamus with you.

SLAM! The whole ring shakes as he crashes into the mat. You cover him for the pin, and he's too stunned to kick out. You've won the match!

Outside the ring, Randy Orton is scowling. His

plan to trick you has backfired. He climbs into the ring and grabs a microphone.

"That's it, Wrench!" he growls. "I'll see you at the WWE Night of Champions, just you and me."

"Actually, I have a different idea."

You'd recognize Mr. McMahon's voice anywhere. His face appears on the big video screen over the arena entrance.

"I didn't approve any title match between you and The Wrench," he tells Randy Orton, and you get a sick feeling. Did you go through all this for nothing?

Mr. McMahon sees the look on your face. "Don't worry, Wrench. You'll still get your shot. You've earned it. But this WWE Championship match is going to be under my terms. I want to see a Fatal 4-Way on the WWE Night of Champions!"

Randy Orton looks angry, but he doesn't complain. "One man, three men—it doesn't make a difference to me," he says. "I am not leaving that event without my championship!"

"You'll have to fight for it," Mr. McMahon says. "Because John Cena and Rey Mysterio want it, too."

The crowd goes crazy. That's a recipe for a great match. You just wonder how you're going to survive in the ring against some of WWE's most talented Superstars.

You spend the days leading up to the match training as hard as you can. Nobody thinks you stand a chance of winning. That doesn't matter. You just have to believe in yourself.

When the WWE Night of Champions starts, you hide out in your dressing room. You need to stay focused, and the Fatal 4-Way will be the last match of the night. When you're finally called to the ring, there's a different Superstar in each corner.

The bell rings, and John Cena and Randy Orton immediately go after each other. That leaves you and Rey Mysterio, the master of high-flying moves.

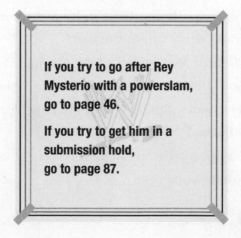

If you try to go after Rey Mysterio with a powerslam, go to page 46.

If you try to get him in a submission hold, go to page 87.

CONTINUED FROM PAGE 79

You charge at Cody Rhodes and whack him with a hard chop to the chest. Then you quickly spin behind him and try to get him in a Cobra Clutch.

But you forget that you're in your opponents' corner, and Ted DiBiase is right behind you! Cody kicks out, hitting the ref, who doubles over in pain. While the ref is looking down, DiBiase sees his chance. He grabs you around the neck, putting a powerful chokehold on you.

The hold weakens you, and when DiBiase lets go, it's easy for Cody Rhodes to wrap his arms around your shoulders and drop you to the mat.

SLAM! Your face smacks into the mat. Cody flips you over and pins you as the ref counts you out.

"Cody Rhodes pins The Wrench! His championship hopes are dashed!"

You sit up, totally crushed. You were so close—but at least you did your best.

THE END

You turn to R-Truth. "Sorry," you say. "But this is something I've got to do."

Then you take a deep breath and walk back onstage, grabbing the mic from Randy Orton midsentence. His steely eyes seem to burn right through you, and you wonder if you've just made the biggest mistake of your life.

But there's no turning back now.

"Randy Orton, you and everyone else in WWE knows that I want to win a championship title at the WWE Night of Champions," you say. "And if I'm gonna do this, I'm gonna do it big. Let me prove myself. Give me a shot at your title!"

The crowd goes silent, and everyone's wondering how Orton will react. Most of them expect him to assault you with an RKO right then and there.

Orton stares at you for a minute. Then, to your surprise, he breaks out into a small smile.

"You are either the bravest or stupidest kid I've ever met," he says. "Tell you what, Wrench. I'll give you a title shot."

The crowd murmurs in disbelief, and you're stunned, too. Randy Orton, a living legend, has accepted your challenge!

"On one condition," Orton continues. "You've got to prove yourself worthy. I'll only face you at WWE Night of Champions if you take down three Superstars of my choice."

You think carefully. This could be the biggest victory of your life—or the biggest humiliation.

If you back out, go to page 27.

If you take Orton's challenge, go to page 75.

Taking on Mark Henry by yourself might be really brave, but it would be really foolish, too. You race to your corner and tag R-Truth.

"Five seconds," he tells you.

You nod back—and then the two of you charge toward Mark Henry. You each grab one shoulder and push.

WHAM! The big man goes down on the mat.

It sounds like a thunderclap, but you can still hear the ref counting you out. You quickly go back to your corner just as he yells, "Five!" You've made it!

Henry's down, and R-Truth is in control. He quickly climbs the ropes and flies down, pinning his body over Mark Henry's. Then he puts all his weight on top of the large Superstar.

"One . . . two . . . three!" the ref counts.

R-Truth jumps up, pumping his fists in the air.

Jerry Lawler is excited. "R-Truth has taken down the World's Strongest Man! He and The Wrench are the last team in the Tag Team Turmoil! R-Truth is amazing!"

You run out into the ring and join R-Truth. He

might be getting all the credit, but you don't care.

You're going to the WWE Night of Champions!

You and R-Truth train hard in the days leading up to the big event. You watch footage of previous Tag Team Turmoil matches so you know what to expect. Four teams will participate. Two teams enter the ring first.

When one team is eliminated because one of the members is counted out or taps out, a second team enters the ring. The match keeps going until only one team is left standing.

The lineup on WWE Night of Champions will be you and R-Truth, the Usos, Cody Rhodes and Ted DiBiase, and the Hart Dynasty. You won't know the order until the match begins.

You're totally pumped when the big night arrives. The Tag Team Turmoil match is the first match of the night. You wait backstage with the other teams, sizing up your competition.

Jimmy and Jey Uso are twin brothers, Samoan Superstars from the same family as The Rock. Standing between them is their friend Tamina, daughter of the legendary high-flier Jimmy Snuka. She's been known to help the brothers in the ring.

Cody Rhodes and Ted DiBiase are also from great wrestling families. They're both dedicated and competitive, and you know their thirst to win is as great as yours.

Then there's the Hart Dynasty tag team. Tyson Kidd may look ridiculous with that tuft of hair sprouting up on his bald head, but he's got a sound technical style. His partner, David Hart Smith, has the same mix of power and agility that his late, great father, Davey Boy Smith, had.

Suddenly the lights in the arena dim. The match is about to start.

"Approaching the ring, from San Francisco, California . . . the Usos!"

Jimmy and Jey nod to each other and then race into the arena as their theme music plays. When the sound of the cheering crowd finally dies down, the announcer reveals the next team out.

"And now for the second team competing in Tag Team Turmoil . . . R-Truth and The Wrench!"

R-Truth grins at you, and the two of you step out into the bright lights. Going out first is exciting, but it puts you at a disadvantage. You're going to have to defeat all three teams if you want the championship.

When the bell rings, R-Truth faces off against Jimmy Uso. The two Superstars exchange powerful punches and kicks. Then R-Truth climbs the ropes, and

Tamina runs up behind and pushes him right off! She runs away before the ref can see her.

This makes you pretty mad. You hate cheating. R-Truth is flat on the mat now, and Jimmy Uso climbs the rope and soars down to cover him. R-Truth rolls out of the way just in time.

He jumps to his feet and races up to you. He doesn't tag you in—but he whispers something to you.

"Take out the ref," he says. "I have a plan."

If you take out the ref,
go to page 28.

If you don't listen to R-Truth,
go to page 77.

You jump up and stand over Punk, who's on his back. You lift up both of his legs by his ankles and step between them, planting your left foot on the mat next to Punk's abdomen. Then you spin around to the left, twisting Punk's legs and pulling them toward you. Now the Straight Edge Superstar is facedown on the mat, and you're in control.

Both of your feet are planted firmly on the mat, and that gives you an advantage. CM Punk tries to break free, but he can't. After a few more seconds, you hear him utter those beautiful words: "I quit!"

The bell rings, and you drop his legs, then charge around the ring, whooping with happiness. You're going to the WWE Night of Champions!

The big event is only a week away.

When you step into the arena, you almost can't believe you're there. You can't remember the last time you felt so excited.

Mr. McMahon wants you to face Drew McIntyre in a Ladder Match. The United States Championship will hang from the ceiling right over the center of the ring. The only way to get it is to climb a tall ladder, which isn't easy to do when your opponent wants the same thing as you.

When it's time for the match, you're called into the ring first. Then the lights dim, and Drew McIntyre's theme song starts. The crowd rises to its feet.

Drew walks down the aisle with a confident smile on his face. He's wearing black trunks, black boots, and his long, brown hair is tied back in a ponytail.

As McIntyre approaches, your eye is drawn to the gold prize hanging right over your head. It's so close . . . but what's the best strategy for getting it?

If you go for the ladder as soon as the bell rings, go to page 15.

If you go for McIntyre instead, go to page 31.

For some reason, you want to save Randy Orton for last. That just seems right.

You charge across the ring at John Cena, and he tries to stop you with a shoulder block. He's got his arms at his sides, and he rams into your shoulder with his. But when you make contact, the move backfires on him, and you take him down.

Cena is an incredible athlete and a champion many times over. But you got lucky—you've got him down on the mat. Now it's time to put one of your trademark submission holds to work.

You quickly stand by Cena's feet and grab a leg in each hand. Then you twist the legs in an impossible position, turn around, and squat, putting pressure on Cena's legs and stretching his spine. It's a classic cloverleaf hold, and you use every ounce of strength you have to keep it on Cena. He tries to kick out, but he can't. The next thing you hear is the sound of the bell. He's tapped out!

You can't believe it. You took out John Cena! Now it's just you and Orton in the ring, staring each other down.

If you try to take him down with a clothesline, go to page 20.

If you try to take him down with a submission hold, like a Cobra Clutch, go to page 92.

Drew McIntyre is laid out flat on the mat, moaning. You race to the nearest corner and climb to the top rope. You raise both arms above your head, and the crowd cheers you on. This is it! Once you knock out McIntyre, you can climb the ladder and grab the United States Championship.

Suddenly, you feel your feet give way beneath you. At first you don't realize what's happening—until you look down and see an angry CM Punk behind you. Before you can react, you fall headfirst onto the arena floor, and your ankles get tangled in the ropes.

"This should be *my* match!" Punk roars angrily. He pulls you off the ropes and then picks you up and slams you into the arena floor again.

This time, you're out cold—for real. When you come to, you see McIntyre standing on top of the ladder! You slide into the ring to stop him, but it's too late. He's grabbed the championship and is waving it in the air victoriously.

You're devastated—but you're angry, too. You grab the mic, interrupting the announcer as he's naming

McIntyre the United States Champion.

"CM Punk, I am coming for you!" you bellow. "You stole my shot at a championship, and I'm going to steal your dignity, your hopes, and your pride!"

You storm out of the ring, furious. It stinks that you didn't get the title. But on the plus side, you've started a rivalry with CM Punk that is hugely popular with the fans. You're not a champion, but you're not a bridesmaid anymore, either.

THE END

Randy Orton might be setting you up for the biggest pain of your life—but you can't back down now. If you do, everyone in WWE will call you a coward.

"Bring it on," you say. "I'll take down anyone I have to if it lands me a shot at the WWE Championship."

Orton gets that smile back on his face. "Think you can handle Big Show?"

You try not to show the panic building up inside you. Big Show is seven feet tall and nearly five hundred pounds. He could chew you up and spit you out in seconds. But you can't show your fear.

"No problem," you say.

"Good," Orton says. "I'll set things up for the next *SmackDown*. Now get out of here before I change my mind."

He doesn't have to ask you twice. You hurry offstage, where R-Truth is shaking his head in disbelief.

"You may not survive this, but at least you'll get noticed," he tells you before turning his back on you and walking away.

You've got about a week to train for the match. The

word around WWE is that it's going to be a bloodbath. You think that's probably true.

Finally, the big night comes. You're warming up backstage when David Otunga and Mason Ryan of The New Nexus approach you.

"We like you, Wrench," says Otunga, a muscular athlete with a clipped black goatee. "Say the word, and we'll back you up tonight."

"What do you mean 'back me up'?" you ask, confused.

Ryan leans in. "We'll interfere," he says in a harsh whisper. "If we don't, Big Show's going to crush you."

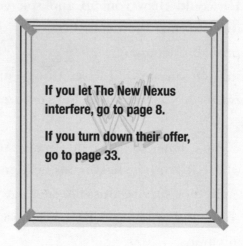

If you let The New Nexus interfere, go to page 8.

If you turn down their offer, go to page 33.

You shake your head no, and R-Truth looks surprised. Then he shrugs and tags you in.

Jimmy Uso has tagged his brother, Jey, and you charge the high-flier, catching him off guard with a clothesline to the chest. You hit him so hard that he hits the ropes behind you and then bounces back at you like a rock in a slingshot. You dodge out of his way and spin around, whacking him on the side of the head with a jumping high kick.

You and Jey go back and forth, but you're not tired at all—it's exhilarating. Jey spins to hit you with a kick, and you grab his leg, pushing him forward. While his back is to you, you grab his neck in a half nelson hold with one hand and wrap your other arm around his waist. Then you leap forward.

BAM! You land in a sitting position, but Jey Uso smacks into the mat facedown. He's dazed by the throw, and you've got him right where you want him. You flip him over and cover him as the ref counts him out.

"One . . . two . . . three!"

You leap up, pumped with excitement. R-Truth

jumps into the ring next to you.

"Great job," he says. "I lost it there for a minute. I was pretty mad when Tamina interfered. I'm glad you kept your head on straight."

"No problem," you say, and you feel proud to have a great Superstar like R-Truth compliment you like this.

The Usos limp away from the ring, and you barely have time to catch your breath before the next tag team is announced.

"Approaching the ring . . . Cody Rhodes and Ted DiBiase!"

Cody and Ted run down the aisle, full of energy. R-Truth gets back in the ring to face them first, and he ends up with Ted DiBiase. The Fortunate Son assaults R-Truth with a punishing elbow drop to the chest. R-Truth doubles over, and DiBiase pummels him with a series of powerful punches.

R-Truth counters by jumping and whacking DiBiase's calf with a powerful kick. Then he grabs a wobbling DiBiase by the shoulders and tosses him against the ropes.

DiBiase tags Cody Rhodes, and R-Truth tags you. You charge after Rhodes, trying to decide your first move.

If you catapult off the ropes and perform a flying lariat, go to page 53.

If you try to get behind Rhodes and get him in a hold, go to page 62.

You grab Punk's right leg and spin around, grabbing his left leg as you go. Then you drop to the mat, applying pressure to Punk's twisted legs. You've been a victim of this hold before, and you know how brutal it is. But is it enough to get Punk to submit?

You've got a good hold on Punk's legs, but he's stronger than you guessed. He pushes up and flips both of you over, and you lose your grip on his legs. He takes advantage of your surprise by slamming you back on the mat and grabbing your leg. You realize he's performing the same move on you!

The pain is excruciating. You try to flip out of the move, like Punk did, but you just can't do it. The Straight Edge Superstar has you in an impossible situation.

"I quit!" you yell, even though it kills you to say the words. CM Punk releases his hold and jumps to his feet, grinning as you try to stretch out your aching legs.

"I knew you'd be easy to beat," he says.

THE END

You've got your eyes on the Intercontinental Championship. Near the end of *SmackDown*, you race into the ring and grab the mic from the announcer.

"Kofi Kingston, the only reason you're in line to face Dolph Ziggler is because I helped you beat Alberto Del Rio!" you say, calling him out. "I deserve one more shot, and you owe it to me."

Kofi enters the arena, his dreadlocks pulled back with a white headband.

"I didn't need your help to beat Del Rio," he calls out to you. "But if you want a title shot, let's do it, if that's what it'll take to get you to shut up."

You're stunned. You've got another chance! "I'll see you next week on *SmackDown*!" you promise.

The crowd goes wild. Backstage, Superstar David Hart Smith is shaking his head.

"That was a crazy move," he tells you. "Kofi's a monster in the ring. You're gonna get pummeled."

"No risk, no reward," you say confidently. But inside, you're starting to doubt yourself. Kingston's mix of high-flying agility and strength is tough to beat.

During the week before the match you train hard. You also read the wrestling blogs every night, and every expert says you're going to lose. By the time the match rolls around, your confidence level is at an all-time low.

The crowd is pumped when you enter the ring, but they go absolutely nuts when Kofi bursts into the arena in a blaze of green-and-yellow light. He races into the ring and goes after you before the bell rings.

SLAM! He hits you hard with a jump kick that sends you flying over the top rope. Then he climbs the rope and covers you with a frog splash as you're lying on the floor groaning.

The Jamaican Sensation totally dominates the match. It's embarrassing. He mercifully finishes you off with his signature move, Trouble in Paradise. He jumps up like Bruce Lee and spins around, aiming a powerful kick at your chin. You're out like a light. When you wake up, the announcer is naming Kofi the winner.

It looks like the Intercontinental Championship is one title you're not destined to win.

THE END

"Double Belly-to-Belly Suplex," you tell R-Truth.

You have to move fast. You've got only five seconds before the ref counts you out. You let go of Kidd's arms and move to the right, putting your head under his right arm.

What's supposed to happen is that R-Truth puts his head under Tyson's left arm, and then the two of you will drop backward, forcing Tyson upside down and driving him into the mat.

But Tyson Kidd is too fast for you. Before R-Truth can get into position, Kidd grabs your neck with his other hand and drives *you* to the mat, nearly knocking you out. He quickly covers you for the pin, and you can't kick out.

"Tyson Kidd and David Hart Smith are the new WWE Tag Team Champions!" the announcer cheers, and the fans clap and whistle. You get up and slowly walk back to R-Truth.

"Sorry, man," you say.

"It's okay," he says. "You did your best."

You don't win the title, and some of the fans won't let you forget it, but most of them do—and you and R-Truth become a hugely popular tag team.

THE END

CONTINUED FROM PAGE 48

You grab the chair and bring it down on Chris Masters's back with a loud smack. He crumples to the floor in a heap. Because it's a Falls Count Anywhere Match, the ref is right there. You act quickly, covering Masters for the pin.

He's out cold. This is almost too easy.

"One . . . two . . . three!"

You jump up and down, pumping the air with your fist. Some of the crowd is booing you—hitting Masters with the chair was a bad guy move. But you don't care. You've taken down two Superstars. One more and you'll get the title shot you want so desperately.

The crowd suddenly gets quiet, and that's when you turn and see Theodore Long enter the ring—with CM Punk by his side.

"It's time for your final match, Wrench," Long tells you, and you can't believe it. Three matches in one night? Mr. McMahon never mentioned that.

CM Punk is sneering. He takes the mic away from Long.

"This is gonna be easy," he calls out. "Why do you

think I helped you before? I'd rather face you than that all-American jerk."

You climb into the ring and face CM Punk, staring him down. Those are fighting words.

Long takes the mic back. "You two are going to be facing each other in an 'I Quit' Match," he tells you.

Normally, that would be good news. In an "I Quit" Match, the only way you can win is if your opponent taps out. A Superstar with strong submission holds like you has an advantage.

But you're coming off two matches, and you're not at 100 percent right now. Also, one of CM Punk's notorious finishing moves is a strong submission hold— the Anaconda Vise.

If you show your fear, you're done. So you put on your best game face.

"Let's do this now!" you shout.

The general manager quickly leaves the ring as you and CM Punk face off. When the bell rings, you try to make the first move, but the Straight Edge Superstar is faster. He spins in a complete circle, finishing with a kick to your chest.

WHAM! The blow rocks your body, and you struggle to stay on your feet. You're going to need to use strategy to win this match, or you won't have a chance.

**If you try to get CM Punk
down on the mat,
go to page 25.**

**If you try to hold him off
until you gain more energy,
go to page 44.**

You try to grab Rey Mysterio in a headlock, but the agile athlete slips right out of it. He quickly climbs to the top rope and flies off like a masked missile, wrapping his legs around your neck. You both crash into the ring, but the impact is much worse on you. The attack leaves you dazed.

Rey covers you and pins you. You try to kick out, but the ref counts to three before you can break free.

You're out of the match! It's exactly what everyone expected. You didn't get the championship you wanted, but you did earn the respect of the fans and fellow Superstars for making it this far.

THE END

Every muscle in your body aches, and you're not thinking clearly. Then your training comes back to you—there's one way to get out of this.

You lean your whole body forward, bringing you and Yoshi Tatsu down on the mat. He loses his hold on you, and you roll to the side, gasping for breath. That was close.

That gets the crowd going. They even start to chant your name. "Wrench! Wrench! Wrench!"

You climb back to your feet and face Yoshi again. He barrages you with a round of martial-arts style kicks, and he's fast. But you're fast, too, and you avoid most of them.

The next time Yoshi throws a kick, you grab his ankle and apply a punishing ankle lock. Then you drop to the mat, pulling Yoshi's leg like a scissor.

He tries to crawl to the ropes, but you don't let him. You want this too much. When Yoshi can't take it anymore, he taps out. You've won your second challenge match!

But before you can celebrate, the arena is bathed in green light, and Sheamus's theme music echoes through the stands. You look to the entrance and see the ghostly pale, redheaded Celtic Warrior stomping toward you.

It's your last challenge, and it won't be easy. Sheamus has been WWE Champion and King of the Ring. He's got a size advantage on you, too.

"Randy Orton sent me!" he snarls, charging at you. The bell rings, and that's when the madness begins.

Sheamus charges at you like an angry rhino, shoving you against the ropes and delivering hard punches to your chest and shoulders. You launch a lot of your attacks from the ropes, hoping to use the extra energy to take down the big man. You manage to get him off his feet a couple of times. You're not winning, but you're holding your own.

Then you hear a familiar voice outside the ring. It's Randy Orton!

"You want to beat me? Then let's do this here and now!" he challenges you.

If you leave the ring to face Orton, go to page 22.

If you stick with Sheamus, go to page 59.

"Why do you want me to join The New Nexus and team with you?" you ask Skip Sheffield.

"Rumor has it that Mr. McMahon is anxious to give you a title shot," Skip replies. "If you do it with R-Truth, everyone will forget about you the next day. For some reason, everybody loves that guy. If you join The New Nexus, everyone will be talking about you again. And I wouldn't mind a title, either."

Sheffield is a two-hundred-and-seventy-pound muscled monster with a shaved, bald head. He's wearing a cowboy hat and vest with his wrestling trunks. He might be called The Cornfed Meathead, but right now he's making a lot of sense.

"All right," you say. "I'll do it."

You give Mr. McMahon a call, and you're surprised when he approves the move. You tell R-Truth in person, and he's not too happy.

"Backing out is just not cool," he says. "But if that's what you think you gotta do . . ."

Your match with Skip Sheffield is set for the next

Raw. You train with Skip, but you don't have the same rhythm you had with R-Truth.

On *Raw*, you face Mark Henry and Evan Bourne. You and Evan are about the same size, and Skip has enough power to hold his own against the mammoth Mark Henry. But during the match, Skip tags you in when Henry is still in the ring. Henry scoops you up and wallops you with a World's Strongest Slam. You don't know what has hit you. He covers you for the pin, and you and Sheffield lose the match.

You call Mr. McMahon and ask for another chance. Can you find another partner and still compete on WWE Night of Champions?

"Sorry, kid," he says. "You've been making some bad decisions lately. I'm sending you back to *SmackDown*."

THE END

You're feeling good about Cena tapping out, so you go for the Cobra Clutch, even though it's risky.

You run up behind Orton and stick your arms under his armpits so you can put him in a half nelson. But you don't get a chance to finish the hold. Orton breaks loose and turns you around so now your back is to him.

He grabs one of your wrists, uses his free hand to grab a leg, and lifts you up above his head. Then he spins and falls to the mat, slamming you into the canvas.

"That was some slam!" Jerry Lawler crows.

The move nearly knocks you out, and when Orton climbs on top of you to pin you, there's no way you can push him off. The bell rings, and you know you've lost.

"Nice try, loser," Orton sneers, but then his expression changes as Mr. McMahon walks into the ring.

"Wrench, you've impressed me," he tells you. "I'm going to let you challenge Orton to a title rematch on the next *Raw*. What do you say?"

You smile. "Yes!"

THE END

You know there's no way you'll ever beat Undertaker.

"I'll try the three specialty matches," you tell Mr. McMahon.

Mr. McMahon nods, pleased. "I gotta give it to you, kid. This is going to be great entertainment. I don't know what's gotten into you, but I like it."

The chairman has never praised you like this before, and it feels good. "Thanks," you say. "So what's the first match?"

Mr. McMahon grins. "You'll find out on the next *SmackDown*."

You can hardly wait to find out what Mr. McMahon has planned for you. When the next *SmackDown* begins, General Manager Theodore Long is interviewed backstage.

"As everyone knows, The Wrench has announced his intention to win a championship," Long begins. "Mr. McMahon has sanctioned The Wrench to wrestle in three matches with three other title contenders. The first one will be held later tonight. Wrench will face Jack

Swagger in a one-fall contest. The winner will go on to WWE Night of Champions. And the loser will have to shave his head!"

So it's Jack Swagger. He's bigger than you, and he's already got a World Heavyweight Championship under his belt. But he's no Undertaker. You just might have a chance. You run your hand through your hair. Will it still be there at the end of the night?

Before you know it, it's time for the match. Jack Swagger confidently walks down the aisle. He's tall, muscled, with blond hair and blue eyes—the All-American.

He's got some words for you before the match starts. "Get ready to lose that fuzz on your head, Wrench. Only a true champion can take down this champion!"

The bell rings, and Swagger throws down the microphone and immediately assaults you with some forceful punches to the head. You counter with a knee to the gut, hoping he'll back off. But he won't stop.

You dodge to the side and dash to the corner of the ring, using the ropes to bounce yourself into Swagger. You crash into him hard, and he falters but doesn't fall.

Swagger's eyes blaze with anger as he fights back with a running knee lift. You see stars as his massive knee smashes into your chin.

While you're dazed, Swagger reaches between your legs and lifts you over his shoulder. You know what's coming—an Oklahoma Stampede.

WHAM! He slams you into one corner of the ring.

BAM! He carries you into the opposite corner and slams you again.

SLAM! He throws you into the center of the ring like a rag doll. You lie there, limp, as he works the crowd into a frenzy.

He's got his back to you. You hear a voice at the side of the ring.

"Hey, Wrench!"

It's CM Punk. The tattooed Superstar says he's straight edge, but he can be as sneaky as a snake in the ring.

"He's decimating you. Say the word, and I'll help you," Punk offers.

You look up at Jack Swagger. Punk is right—he's dominating the match. But why does Punk want to help you?

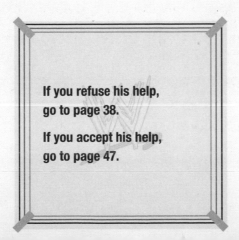

If you refuse his help,
go to page 38.

If you accept his help,
go to page 47.